Lila Lou's Little Library

A Gift From the Heart

By Nikki Bergstresser

Illustrated by Sejung Kim

Lila Lou's Little Library

Copyright 2020 by Nikki Bergstresser
All rights reserved. First Edition
Printed in China

Summary: Lila Lou has a plan to share her love of books with the neighborhood.

Our books may be purchased in bulk for promotional, educational or business use. Please contact your local bookseller or IPG Books at orders@ipgbook.com

This book was edited by a sensitivity reader in the Latinx community to help guide our team in appropriately representing the culture.

Library of CongressControl Number: 2020941583
ISBN (hardcover) ISBN: 978-1-7353451-1-6
ISBN (ebook) ISBN: 978-1-7353451-0-9

The art in this book was created using Adobe photoshop and a Wacom tablet.

Book design by: Maggie Villaume

Cardinal Rule Press
5449 Sylvia
Dearborn Heights, MI 48125
Visit us at www.CardinalRulePress.com

Before Reading

- Read the title of the book.
- Ask your child what they think a little library looks like.
- Discuss ways they have shared books with others.
- What are two books you would share with others? Why did you choose those books?

While Reading

- Talk about the places where Lila Lou reads. Ask your child where their favorite places are to read.
- Lila Lou had an idea that grew. Talk about how an idea can grow.
- Lila Lou has a problem when no one notices her little library. Talk about how she did not give up. Ask your child if they could think of another way Lila Lou could have gotten others to notice her library.

After Reading

- Ask your child for some ideas on why Lila Lou was happy at the end of the story.
- With your child, look up some examples of different styles of little libraries online.
- Using colored pencils and paper, have your child design their own little library.
- Find out if there are any little libraries in your town and plan an adventure to visit one together.

For my family, who gave me wings to dream.
And for my friends, who share a love of books.

NIKKI BERGSTRESSER

For my son, Loan.

SEJUNG KIM

Lila Lou loved to read. Morning, noon, and night, her nose was buried in a book.

Books piled here, books piled there. In every
nook and cranny, books were piled everywhere.
Lila Lou would even get lost in her books.

"Lila Lou?" called out her mom.

"Over here!" came a voice from among all the books.

Giving a sigh, her mom looked under, climbed over, and squeezed past the stacks of books. "Where are you?"

"Over here!"

"Where?"

"Here!"

She finally found Lila Lou reading
in a fort...made from books!

Her mom crossed her arms and shook her head.

Lila Lou knew the words that would come
from her mom's mouth next.

"Lila Lou, there are too many books in this house!"

"Maybe our house is just too small for all these books?"
Lila Lou winked and grinned.

RUMBLE. RUMBLE. RUMBLE. RUMBLE.

From deep inside the closet door, the noise grew and grew. Lila Lou's mom slowly opened the door and peeked inside. She opened it a little further. A pile of books came tumbling down!

"I guess I could share my books with others,"
Lila Lou quickly suggested.

That day Lila Lou had an idea that grew and grew.
She gathered her glitter and her glue.

She grabbed a hammer, nails, and paint.
Lastly, she grabbed her mom and headed outside.

In Lila Lou's front yard stood the largest tree stump ever. Lila Lou had been sad when the old oak tree fell during a storm last winter. But now, a smile spread across her face. She threw her arms around the stump and gave it a hug.

"This is the perfect place!"

Her mom looked confused. "For what, Lila Lou?"

"You will see. Let's get to work!"

BANG BAM BUZZ

CLATTER CLANG CLANK

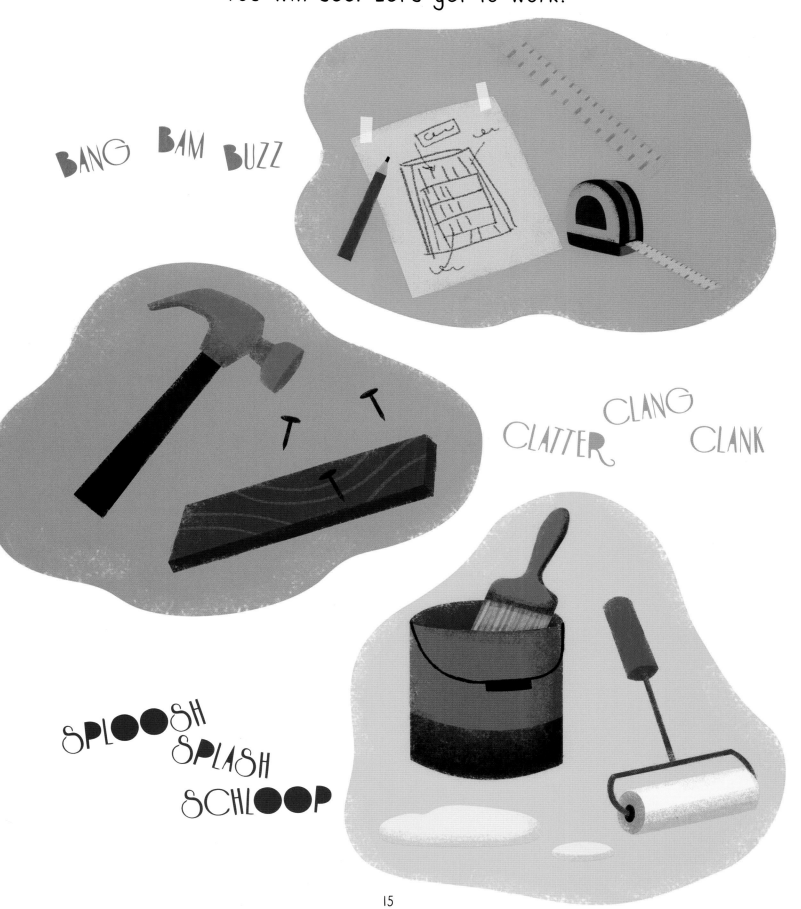

SPLOOSH SPLASH SCHLOOP

Lila Lou and her mom worked till dusk. The sun was setting when they hung the sign on the tree stump. Lila Lou and her mom stood back and admired the work.

"I think this will do," Lila Lou smiled.
"I think this will, too," Her mom wiped her brow.
The sign above the stump read, *"Lila Lou's Little Library."*

From all around her house, Lila Lou gathered books. Books about frogs, purple-striped monsters, beautiful butterflies, lands far away, princesses, fierce dragons, and other creatures.

She stacked her books neatly on
bookshelves on the tree stump.

Lila Lou was up with the sunshine and birds the next morning to see who would visit her library. She sat by the tree stump and waited. And she waited.

Nobody came. People walked by, but no one noticed her library.

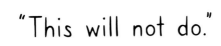

"This will not do."

Lila Lou crossed her arms and thought.

She raced into her garage and brought out an old bell from a bicycle.

It sounded just like the ice cream truck that drove around the neighborhood.

Ting-a-ling! Ting-a-ling! Ting-a-ling!

Soon a curious crowd gathered.

Lila Lou scrambled up to the tippy top of the pile on the stump.

"My books are magical, wait and see.

Pick one, pick two, or even three.

They will take you to places--adventures galore!

When you spend time with books,
you will want to read more!"

Lila Lou's
Little Library

EVIE'S FIELD DAY

LA GEOGRAFIA

Dazzling Travis

Conexión en un pasillo de perro caliente

Kindness is a Kite String

EL PERRO BLANCO

EL DIA SOLEADO

El reloje música

MATEMATICAS

"Can I have a book?" asked a boy with his dog.
"Do you have one for my baby?" asked a woman pushing a stroller.

"We want books, too!" called some others.

Soon the entire neighborhood was borrowing books, leaving books, and lending books at Lila Lou's Little Library.

Not only did they always have a new book to read, but so did Lila Lou!

BUILDING
a family Library

THE SPACE

- Choose a quiet place in your home away from distractions.

- Fill your book nook with cozy pillows to snuggle and stuffed animals as reading buddies.

- Designate a wooden crate or sturdy box to contain all borrowed library books for easy access. Paint and decorate your library container.

THE BOOKS

- Include a variety of reading genres on your book shelves from fiction to nonfiction.

- Keep one shelf for "seasonal or holiday" books or family favorites that can be rotated. These books could be kept in storage until it is time to share them. It builds an anticipation of beloved books returning to the shelf.

BEYOND THE BOOK

- Make a "Share It" station to keep blank paper, cardstock, coloring, and writing utensils where children could make book posters or bookmarks. Letters to authors or book reviews could be written, too.

- Plan special times around the family library space. Set up a fort and read stories by flashlights together. Or on a rainy day, spread out a picnic blanket and enjoy a picnic lunch while reading together. Host a "Poetry and Tea" time.

- As a family, go through your library shelves and tidy together. Decide on books you would like to donate to little libraries around your neighborhood. Make your family library work for your family. It will change as your family grows.

HOW TO GROW your Library

- Visit your library on a regular basis to borrow books.

- Go on treasure quests with your family to find books at garage sales, flea markets, thrift stores or library book sales.

- Host a book swap party with neighbors or friends.

- Ask family members to give books or magazine subscriptions as gifts.

- Follow authors and publishers on social media and participate in book giveaways.

NIKKI BERGSTRESSER

Nikki Bergstresser is the author of *Seasons for Stones* and *Lila Lou's Little Library*. She lives on the west coast of British Columbia, Canada, with her husband and two daughters. Nikki can be found surrounded by books and a good story to share.

SEJUNG KIM

Sejung Kim is an illustrator and author who was born in South Korea and now lives and works in France. She often works in early childhood and has collaborated with many French publishing houses. She continues to create beautiful projects that are inspiring for young and old alike.

SPANISH GLOSSARY